Moving Day for Alex

The first book in the *Growing Up with Alex* series

by Cynthia MacGregor

illustrations by Tracie Mitchell

D1278567

Acknowledgments

I would like to thank the entire AbyD team, especially talented illustrator Tracie Mitchell and equally talented layout artist, AbyD's Art Director Niki Key, also Laurel Tuohy, but particularly AbyD publisher Michel Marion, for coaxing Alex to life and suggesting not just one book but a series. You guys are the greatest! Hugs to you all from this very grateful author.

ACUTE BY DESIGN

the little book company that could

AcuteByDesign is a teeny, tiny book publishing
company with a big mission:

To produce and publish high quality diverse,
multicultural, and socially relevant
books for children and young readers;
their teachers, and parents

To provide opportunities for teachers and
under-represented writers and illustrators to
publish their dream book, and

To provide small grants to teachers and
parent associations to help provide resources
for underserved students and classrooms.

Thank you for helping to make that dream come true for so many!

www.acutebydesign.com

That Saturday started like any other Saturday for Alex Morales. He and his mom got into their big blue van to do errands while Dad mowed the lawn.

When they got home, Alex went out in the backyard to play. He had a swing in the backyard and loved to play on it. Alex's family's house was just down the street from a big park with a playground. Alex's mom often took him there.

He loved to climb on the monkey bars and slide down the slide. But it was still nice to have a swing of his own right in his own yard.

Mom opened the back door to call Alex in to eat his lunch. Her eyes grew wide with concern as Alex jumped from the swing before it had fully stopped.

Alex was unhappy that he had to stop swinging. However, he quickly cheered up when lunch turned out to be one of his favorites: grilled cheese and bacon sandwiches. It was just an ordinary Saturday, but it was a good one, Alex thought, as he munched on his sandwich.

The first sour note on an otherwise sweet day came not long after lunch. Alex asked, "Mom, Dad, can we set up my electric trains this afternoon? I want to play with them."

"Not today, honey," Mom said. Alex frowned.

"That's not fair. My friend Evan gets to keep his electric trains set up all the time." Alex scrunched up his face and raised his voice. "He can play with his trains whenever he wants, and I can't."

"Alex, we have discussed this before, and you know our house is too small. We'd have to keep stepping over your train set."

Alex's room was certainly too small. The only place in the house to put the train tracks was on the living room floor, and there really wasn't much room there, either.

Alex wasn't happy that his mom and dad wouldn't let him set up his trains today. He stuck out his lower lip. Now it didn't feel like such a good day.

"Don't pout!" Mom told him. But that just made him more unhappy. "You can color in your coloring book," Mom suggested.

"Make a nice picture for me," Dad said. Usually Alex liked to color. But today he really wanted to play with his trains!

Finally it got to be dinnertime. Alex finished his dinner first and asked to be excused to go play. "Please stick around," Dad said. "We're having a family meeting after we all finish eating."

Alex was restless, and he felt himself getting angry. He counted to ten like his father had taught him to do when he felt angry. That only helped a little, but he waited as he had been asked to do. Alex began to wonder what the family meeting was about. It was usually some big announcement. Were they getting another new car? Were they going to visit Grandma and Grandpa?

When the dishes had finally been cleared, Dad said, "It's time for the Morales family meeting." Alex waited to hear what his parents had to say.

"We have big news," Mom and Dad both said at the same time. "What is it?" Alex asked.

"In just three weeks there's going to be a big truck here," Mom started. Alex grinned, and his eyes opened wide. He loved big trucks.

"And it's going to take all our furniture and clothes and your toys and everything we own to a new house," Dad chimed in.

"We're moving," Mom finished. Alex stopped grinning. Mom and Dad looked so happy. But this wasn't good news at all. Moving? Alex began to cry. "I like this house. I don't want to leave my swing set. I don't want to live anywhere else. Why do we have to move?"

"We're moving to a bigger, better, nicer house," Mom said. "You'll love it!"

But Alex was sure he wouldn't. In fact, he was sure he would hate it.

"I don't want to move!" he shouted. Then he kicked the leg of his chair. He kicked it again.

"Please stop that," Mom said quietly but firmly.

"I DON'T WANT TO MOVE!" Alex yelled.

Dad got up from his chair and came around to Alex's seat. He put his arm around Alex. "I understand," Dad said. "It's hard to give up what's familiar. New experiences can be difficult to deal with at first."

"But I'm sure you'll love the new house," Mom added. "And there's a boy your age who lives right next door."

That got Alex's attention. But he still wasn't happy about having to live somewhere new and different. Different was scary.

"I thought you liked adventures," Dad said. "Moving will be a big adventure. Living on a new street in a new house...and I promise there will be a surprise for you too."

"A surprise? A pony?" Alex asked. Now he was getting excited.

"No. It's not a pony," Dad said, laughing. "But I promise you it's something good."

"I want a pony!" Alex said.

"No pony," Dad said firmly. "But I promise you you'll love the surprise anyhow." Dad chuckled.

"Tell me what it is," Alex begged.

"No. You'll just have to wait until we move," Dad said.

"I don't want to move," Alex said again. "I like it here."

"Dad and I like it here too. But we're going to like the new house even better—and so will you," Mom said.

"Do you have any more bad news?" Alex asked.

His mother sighed. "No. The meeting's over," she said. "You may be excused if you want."

Over the next three weeks, more and more big boxes appeared in the house. Some of them were medium size, but some of them were huge—big enough for Alex to fit inside. Mom let Alex play in the big empty boxes. Alex had to admit that was fun.

Every time he played on his backyard swing, he thought about how much he was going to miss swinging in the backyard once they moved.

Finally the big day came. Alex felt sad and just a little bit scared. He hid in his room and cried. One of the moving men came in to get the boxes from his room. He saw Alex crying.

"What's the matter, little dude?" he asked. "You don't want to move?" Alex shook his head. "I've helped lots of families move. "And sometimes the kids aren't happy about it. Just like you. But you know what? Usually they love their new house once they get used to it. I bet you will too.

"Now come on downstairs, and you can watch us load your things into the truck." Alex stopped crying. Watching the truck get loaded might be fun. Alex followed the worker downstairs.

Alex watched as the three workers loaded the cartons into the truck. Then came the furniture. But Alex didn't see his bed go onto the truck. He ran to Dad.

"They forgot my bed!" he said.

"No. We're not bringing it with us," Dad said.

"Do I have to sleep on the floor in the new house?" Alex asked.

Dad laughed. "Your new bed is already waiting for you in your new room," he said.

"New bed?" Alex asked.

"A double-decker," Dad said.

"A bunk bed," Mom said.

"So you can have friends over for sleep-overs." Now Alex was getting excited.

"Can I sleep in the top bed?" he asked.

"Absolutely," Dad said. Alex got even more excited.

"Is that the surprise you promised me?" he asked.

"Nope," Dad said.

"There's something else?" Alex asked.

"Yes," Mom said, nodding her head.

"What is it?" Alex asked.

"You'll see soon enough," Dad told him.

Dad went ahead in his car so he could show the movers where to put everything in the new house. Meanwhile Mom took Alex out for lunch. And after lunch she took him to his favorite ice cream store.

When they got to the new house, the movers still were unloading the big van. Alex wanted to run inside and see the new house. Then again, it was cool to stand outside and watch the movers carrying the heavy cartons and furniture out of the big truck.

Mom suggested to Alex, "Why don't we go check out the backyard? That's where your surprise is."

Alex's face lit up, and he raced around to his new backyard. It was a nice, big backyard. A huge tree grew right in the middle of it. There was even a backyard slide. But Alex missed his swing.

Then he walked partway around the huge tree. Nailed into the tree was a ladder. And when Alex looked up, way up in the tree, he saw that the ladder led to a treehouse! Oh boy, a real treehouse! Alex thought that was the coolest thing ever. He called to his mother, "Is this my surprise?"

Dad was now outside too, and he answered, "Yes! That's your surprise."

Both Mom and Dad smiled to see that Alex was so happy with his new treehouse. "Can I go up into it now?" he asked.

"Let me watch and make sure you climb up safely," Dad answered. Both Mom and Dad stood beneath the ladder as Alex happily climbed up into the treehouse. He stayed up there a long time, playing. Mom sat in a lawn chair, waiting to make sure he could climb down safely.

A long time later, the movers finally finished. At last Alex was able to go into the house. It looked like there was an extra living room downstairs. It was quite large. "That's called a family room," Mom said, "and there's another surprise for you there."

Alex raced into the room and grinned widely when he saw his electric trains set up in the corner of the room. He jumped up and down with excitement. "Can we leave them set up all the time?"

"Yes, we can," Mom said.

"This may be the best house ever. It can't get any better than this!" Alex thought.

Just then the doorbell rang. Alex followed Mom to the door. When Mom opened the door, Alex saw a boy his age standing there.

"Hi," the boy said to him. "Are you Alex? My mom said you were moving in today. I'm DeShawn. I live next door. May I come in?"

Alex looked at Mom. "Sure!" said Mom. Alex didn't waste a moment. He pulled DeShawn toward the family room to check out his train set-up.

All that DeShawn could say was, "Cool!" Both boys began playing with the train set.

Alex's parents walked into the family room. Alex looked over at them, smiled, and said, "This is the best house ever!"

Peacefully,

The End

About the Author

Prolific author Cynthia MacGregor has written over 100 fiction and nonfiction books for both children and adults, more information on which can be found on her website, www.cynthiamacgregor.com.

She has produced and hosted two TV shows, *Solo Parenting* and *Younger Every Day*, both of which aired on WHDT in the South Florida viewing area. She was the number-two finalist one year at the O. Henry Pun-Off World Championships, an annual wordplay competition, where more recently she has been tapped to be one of the judges.

After having several of her books accepted for publication by AcuteByDesign, Cyn (as she likes to be called) agreed to be part of the AbyD "team," serving in editorial and other capacities.

Cynthia absolutely loves her work, and she is emphatic when she says, "I can't wait to bound out of bed in the mornings and get started. I might be the happiest person in the world. There's no one in the world I'd want to trade lives with."

Look for the next two of Cynthia MacGregor's exciting children's stories in the Growing Up with Alex series:

What's So Cool About Starting School?
Alex and the Angries

as well as a new and very special Christmas story:
Heartfelt, the Special Reindeer

You can get in touch with Cynthia at
cynthia@cynthiamacgregor.com

CPSIA information can be obtained at www.ICGtesting.com
Printed in the USA
LVOW05*1816280915

456070LV00018B/172/P